Now We Are Seventy-five

A.A. Milne

Decorations by E.H. Shepard

METH

First published in 2001
Printed under the Methuen imprint
by Egmont Children's Books Limited
a division of Egmont Holding Limited
239 Kensington High Street
London W8 6SA

Now We Are Seventy-five is a collection of previously
published material taken from
When We Were Very Young, first published 26 November 1924
text by A.A.Milne and line illustrations by E.H.Shepard
copyright under the Berne Convention
Winnie-the-Pooh, first published 14 October 1926
text by A.A.Milne and line illustrations by E.H.Shepard
copyright under the Berne Convention
Now We Are Six, first published 13 October 1927
text by A.A.Milne and line illustrations by E.H.Shepard
copyright under the Berne Convention
The House at Pooh Corner, first published 11 October 1928
text by A.A.Milne and line illustrations by E.H.Shepard
copyright under the Berne Convention

1 3 5 7 9 10 8 6 4 2

ISBN 0 416 19927 5

Printed and Bound in Great Britain
by Cox and Wyman

Contents

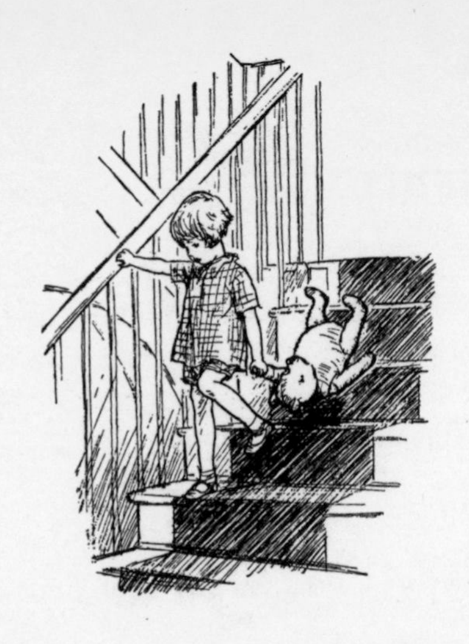

In which we are introduced to Winnie-the-Pooh and some Bees

Here is Edward Bear, coming downstairs now, bump, bump, bump, on the back of his head, behind Christopher Robin. It is, as far as he knows, the only way of coming downstairs, but sometimes he feels that there really is another way, if only he could stop bumping for a moment and think of it. And then he feels that perhaps there isn't. Anyhow, here he is at the bottom, and ready to be introduced to you. Winnie-the-Pooh.

When I first heard his name, I said, just as you are going to say, "But I thought he was a boy?"

"So did I," said Christopher Robin.

"Then you can't call him Winnie?"

"I don't."

"But you said —"

"He's Winnie-ther-Pooh. Don't you know what *'ther'* means?"

"Ah, yes, now I do," I said quickly; and I hope you do too, because it is all the explanation you are going to get.

Sometimes Winnie-the-Pooh likes a game of some sort when he comes downstairs, and sometimes he likes to sit quietly in front of the fire and listen to a story. This evening —

"What about a story?" said Christopher Robin.

"*What* about a story?" I said.

"Could you very sweetly tell Winnie-the-Pooh one?"

"I suppose I could," I said. "What sort of stories does he like?"

"About himself. Because he's *that* sort of Bear."

"Oh, I see."

"So could you very sweetly?"

"I'll try," I said. So I tried.

Once upon a time, a very long time ago now, about last Friday, Winnie-the-Pooh lived in a forest all by himself under the name of Sanders.

("What does 'under the name' mean?" asked Christopher Robin.

"It means he had the name over the door in gold letters and lived under it."

"Winnie-the-Pooh wasn't quite sure," said Christopher Robin.

"Now I am," said a growly voice.

"Then I will go on," said I.)

One day when he was out walking, he came to an open place in the middle of the forest, and in the middle of this place was a large oak-tree, and, from the top of the tree, there came a loud buzzing-noise.

Winnie-the-Pooh sat down at the foot of the tree, put his head between his paws, and began to think.

First of all he said to himself: "That buzzing-noise means something. You don't get a buzzing-noise like that, just buzzing and buzzing, without its meaning something. If there's a buzzing-noise, somebody's making a buzzing-noise, and the only reason for making a buzzing-noise that *I* know of is because you're a bee."

Then he thought another long time, and said: "And the only reason for being a bee that I know of is making honey."

And then he got up, and said: "And the only reason for making honey is so as *I* can eat it." So he began to climb the tree.

He climbed and he climbed and he climbed, and as he climbed he sang a little song to himself. It went like this:

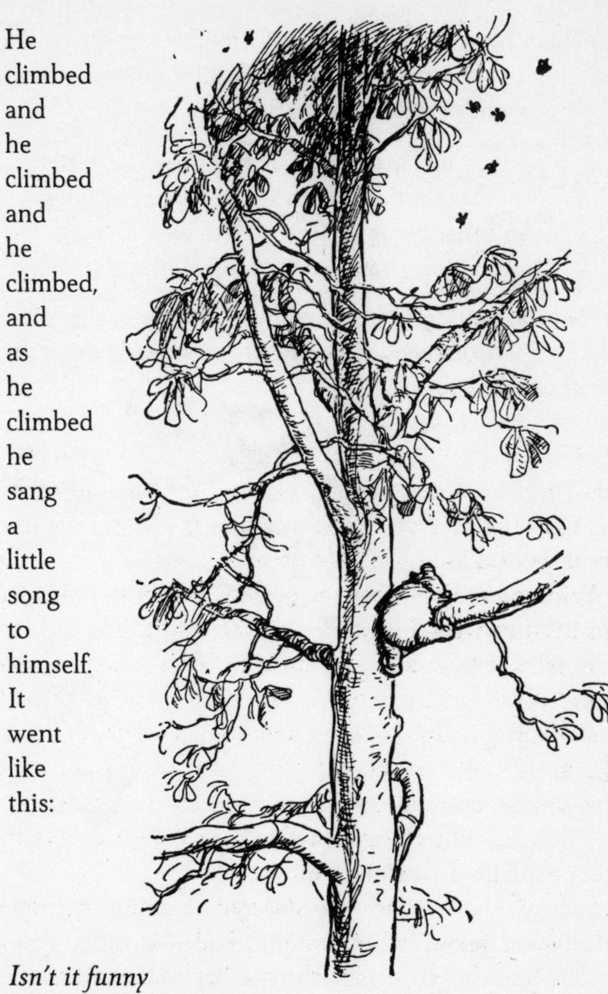

Isn't it funny
How a bear likes honey?
Buzz! Buzz! Buzz!
I wonder why he does?

Then he climbed a little further . . . and a little further . . . and then just a little further. By that time he had thought of another song.

It's a very funny thought that, if Bears were Bees,
They'd build their nests at the *bottom* of trees.
And that being so (if the Bees were Bears),
We shouldn't have to climb up all these stairs.

He was getting rather tired by this time, so that is why he sang a Complaining Song. He was nearly there now, and if he just stood on that branch . . .

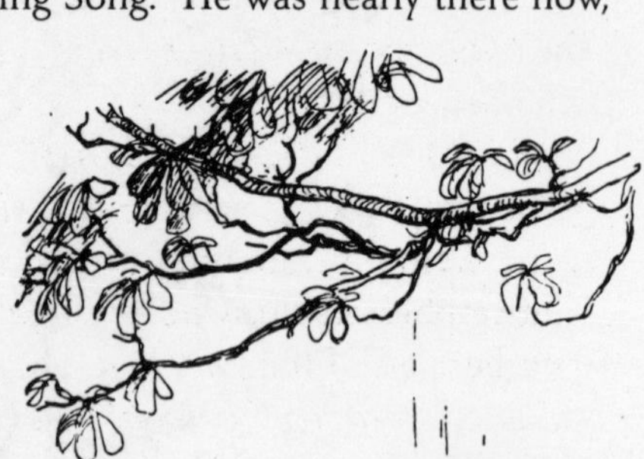

Crack!

"Oh, help!" said Pooh, as he dropped ten feet to the branch below him.

"If only I hadn't —" he said, as he bounced twenty feet on to the next branch.

"You see, what I *meant* to do," he explained, as he turned head-over-heels, and crashed on to another branch thirty feet below, "what I *meant* to do —"

"Of course, it *was* rather—" he admitted, as he slithered very quickly through the next six branches.

"It all comes, I suppose," he decided, as he said good-bye to the last branch, spun round three times, and flew gracefully into a gorse-bush, "it all comes of *liking* honey so much. Oh, help!"

He crawled out of the gorse-bush, brushed the prickles from his nose, and began to think again. And the first person he thought of was Christopher Robin.

("Was that me?" said Christopher Robin in an awed voice, hardly daring to believe it.

"That was you."

Christopher Robin said nothing, but his eyes got larger and larger, and his face got pinker and pinker.)

So Winnie-the-Pooh went round to his friend Christopher Robin, who lived behind a green door in another part of the Forest.

"Good morning, Christopher Robin," he said.

"Good morning, Winnie-*ther*-Pooh," said you.

"I wonder if you've got such a thing as a balloon about you?"

"A balloon?"

"Yes, I just said to myself coming along: 'I wonder if Christopher Robin has such a thing as a balloon about him?' I just said it to myself, thinking of balloons, and wondering."

"What do you want a balloon for?" you said.

Winnie-the-Pooh looked round to see that nobody was listening, put his paw to his mouth, and said in a deep whisper: *"Honey!"*

"But you don't get honey with balloons!"

"*I* do," said Pooh.

Well, it just happened that you had been to a party the

day before at the house of your friend Piglet, and you had balloons at the party. You had had a big green balloon; and one of Rabbit's relations had had a big blue one, and had left it behind, being really too young to go to a party at all; and so you had brought the green one *and* the blue one home with you.

"Which one would you like?" you asked Pooh.

He put his head between his paws and thought very carefully.

"It's like this," he said. "When you go after honey with a balloon, the great thing is not to let the bees know you're coming. Now, if you have a green balloon, they might think you were only part of the tree, and not notice you, and if you have a blue balloon, they might think you were only part of the sky, and not notice you, and the question is: Which is most likely?"

"Wouldn't they notice *you* underneath the balloon?" you asked.

"They might or they might not," said Winnie-the-Pooh. "You never can tell with bees." He thought for a moment and said: "I shall try to look like a small black cloud. That will deceive them."

"Then you had better have the blue balloon," you said; and so it was decided.

Well, you both went out with the blue balloon, and you took your gun with you, just in case, as you always did, and Winnie-the-Pooh went to a very muddy place

that he knew of, and rolled and rolled until he was black all over; and then, when the balloon was blown up as big as big, and you and Pooh were both holding on to the string, you let go suddenly, and Pooh Bear floated gracefully up into the sky, and stayed there – level with the top of the tree and about twenty feet away from it.

"Hooray!" you shouted.

"Isn't that fine?" shouted Winnie-the-Pooh down to you. "What do I look like?"

"You look like a bear holding on to a balloon," you said.

"Not," said Pooh anxiously, " – not like a small black cloud in a blue sky?"

"Not very much."

"Ah, well, perhaps from up here it looks different. And, as I say, you never can tell with bees."

There was no wind to blow him nearer to the tree so there he stayed. He could see the honey, he could smell the honey, but he couldn't quite reach the honey.

After a little while he called down to you.

"Christopher Robin!" he said in a loud whisper.

"Hallo!"

"I think the bees *suspect* something!"

"What sort of thing?"

"I don't know. But something tells me that they're *suspicious*!"

"Perhaps they think that you're after their honey?"

"It may be that. You never can tell with bees."

There was another little silence, and then he called down to you again.

"Christopher Robin!"

"Yes?"

"Have you an umbrella in your house?"

"I think so."

"I wish you would bring it out here, and walk up and down with it, and look up at me every now and then, and say 'Tut-tut, it looks like rain.' I think, if you did that, it would help the deception which we are practising on these bees."

Well, you laughed to yourself, "Silly old Bear!" but you didn't say it aloud because you were so fond of him, and you went home for your umbrella.

"Oh, there you are!" called down Winnie-the-Pooh, as soon as you got back to the tree. "I was beginning to get anxious. I have discovered that the bees are now definitely Suspicious."

"Shall I put my umbrella up?" you said.

"Yes, but wait a moment. We must be practical. The important bee to deceive is the Queen Bee. Can you see which is the Queen Bee from down there?"

"No."

"A pity. Well, now, if you walk up and down with your umbrella, saying, 'Tut-tut, it looks like rain,' I shall do what I can by singing a little Cloud Song, such as a cloud might sing. . . . Go!"

So while you walked up and down and wondered if it would rain, Winnie-the-Pooh sang this song:

How sweet to be a Cloud
Floating in the Blue!
Every little cloud
Always sings aloud.

"How sweet to be a Cloud
Floating in the Blue!"
It makes him very proud
To be a little cloud.

The bees were still buzzing as suspiciously as ever. Some of them, indeed, left their nests and flew all round the cloud as it began the second verse of this song, and one bee sat down on the nose of the cloud for a moment, and then got up again.

"Christopher – *ow!* – Robin," called out the cloud.

"Yes?"

"I have just been thinking, and I have come to a very important decision. *These are the wrong sort of bees.*"

"Are they?"

"Quite the wrong sort. So I should think they would make the wrong sort of honey, shouldn't you?"

"Would they?"

"Yes. So I think I shall come down."

"How?" asked you.

Winnie-the-Pooh hadn't thought about this. If he let go of the string, he would fall – *bump* – and he didn't like the idea of that. So he thought for a long time, and then he said:

"Christopher Robin, you must shoot the balloon with your gun. Have you got your gun?"

"Of course I have," you said. "But if I do that, it will spoil the balloon," you said.

"But if you *don't,*" said Pooh, "I shall have to let go, and that would spoil *me.*"

When he put it like this, you saw how it was, and you aimed very carefully at the balloon, and fired.

"*Ow!*" said Pooh.

"Did I miss?" you asked.

"You didn't exactly *miss,*" said Pooh, "but you missed the *balloon.*"

"I'm so sorry," you said, and you fired again, and this time you hit the balloon, and the air came slowly out, and Winnie-the-Pooh floated down to the ground.

But his arms were so stiff from holding on to the string of the balloon all that time that they stayed up straight in the air for more than a week, and whenever a fly came and settled on his nose he had to blow it off.

And I think – but I am not sure – that that is why he was always called Pooh.

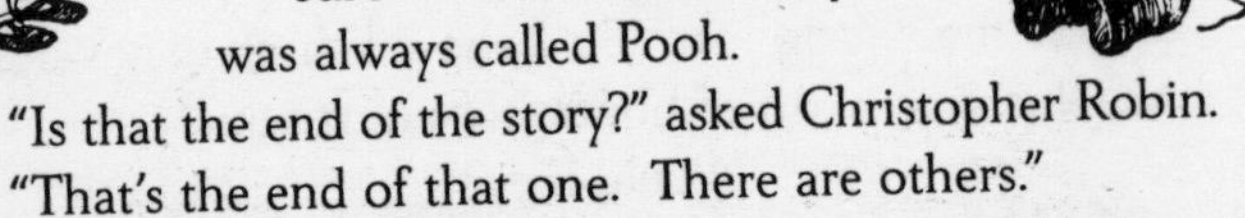

"Is that the end of the story?" asked Christopher Robin.

"That's the end of that one. There are others."

"About Pooh and Me?"

"And Piglet and Rabbit and all of you. Don't you remember?"

"I do remember, and then when I try to remember, I forget."

"That day when Pooh and Piglet tried to catch the Heffalump –"

"They didn't catch it, did they?"

"No."

"Pooh couldn't because he hasn't any brain. Did *I* catch it?"

"Well, that comes into the story."

Christopher Robin nodded.

"I do remember," he said, "only Pooh doesn't very well, so that's why he likes having it told to him again. Because then it's a real story and not just a remembering."

"That's just how *I* feel," I said.

Christopher Robin gave a deep sigh, picked his Bear up by the leg, and walked off to the door, trailing Pooh behind him. At the door he turned and said, "Coming to see me have my bath?"

"I might," I said.

"I didn't hurt him when I shot him, did I?"

"Not a bit."

He nodded and went out, and in a moment I heard Winnie-the-Pooh – *bump, bump, bump* – going up the stairs behind him.

Lines and Squares

Whenever I walk in a London Street,
I'm ever so careful to watch my feet;
  And I keep in the squares,
  And the masses of bears,
Who wait at the corners all ready to eat
The sillies who tread on the lines of the street,
  Go back to their lairs,
  And I say to them, "Bears,
Just look how I'm walking in all the squares!"

And the little bears growl to each other, "He's mine,
As soon as he's silly and steps on a line."
And some of the bigger bears try to pretend
That they came round the corner to look for a friend;
And they try to pretend that nobody cares
Whether you walk on the lines or the squares.
But only the sillies believe their talk;
It's ever so portant how you walk.
And it's ever so jolly to call out, "Bears,
Just watch me walking in all the squares!"

Growing up

I've got shoes with grown-up laces,
I've got knickers and a pair of braces,
I'm all ready to run some races,
Who's coming out with me?

I've got a nice new pair of braces,
I've got shoes with new brown laces,
I know some wonderful paddly places,
Who's coming out with me?

Every morning my new grace is,
"Thank you, God for my new braces;
I can tie my new brown laces."
Who's coming out with me?

In which Eeyore loses a tail and Pooh finds one

The Old Grey Donkey, Eeyore, stood by himself in a thistly corner of the Forest, his front feet well apart, his head on one side, and thought about things. Sometimes he thought sadly to himself, "Why?" and sometimes he thought, "Wherefore?" and sometimes he thought, "Inasmuch as which?" – and sometimes he didn't quite know what he *was* thinking about. So when Winnie-the-Pooh came stumping along, Eeyore was very glad to be able to stop thinking for a little, in order to say "How do you do?" in a gloomy manner to him.

"And how are you?" said Winnie-the-Pooh.

Eeyore shook his head from side to side.

"Not very how," he said. "I don't seem to have felt at all how for a long time."

"Dear, dear," said Pooh, "I'm sorry about that. Let's have a look at you."

So Eeyore stood there, gazing sadly at the ground, and Winnie-the-Pooh walked all round him once.

"Why, what's happened to your tail?" he said in surprise.

"What *has* happened to it?" said Eeyore.

"It isn't there!"

"Are you sure?"

"Well, either a tail *is* there or it isn't there. You can't make a mistake about it, and yours *isn't* there!"

"Then what is?"

"Nothing."

"Let's have a look," said Eeyore, and he turned slowly round to the place where his tail had been a little while ago, and then, finding that he couldn't catch it up, he turned round the other way, until he came back to where he was at first, and then he put his head down and looked between his front legs, and at last he said, with a long, sad sigh, "I believe you're right."

"Of course I'm right," said Pooh.

"That Accounts for a Good Deal," said Eeyore gloomily. "It Explains Everything. No Wonder."

"You must have left it somewhere," said Winnie-the-Pooh.

"Somebody must have taken it," said Eeyore. "How Like Them," he added, after a long silence.

Pooh felt that he ought to say something helpful about it, but didn't quite know what. So he decided to do something helpful instead.

"Eeyore," he said solemnly, "I, Winnie-the-Pooh, will find your tail for you."

"Thank you, Pooh," answered Eeyore. "You're a real

friend," said he. "Not Like Some," he said.

So Winnie-the-Pooh went off to find Eeyore's tail.

It was a fine spring morning in the Forest as he started out. Little soft clouds played happily in a blue sky, skipping from time to time in front of the sun as if they had come to put it out, and then sliding away suddenly so that the next might have his turn. Through them and between them the sun shone bravely; and a copse which had worn its firs all the year round seemed old and dowdy now beside the new green lace which the beeches had put on so prettily. Through copse and spinney marched Bear; down open slopes of gorse and heather, over rocky beds of streams, up steep banks of sandstone into the heather again; and so at last, tired and hungry, to the Hundred Acre Wood. For it was in the Hundred Acre Wood that Owl lived.

"And if anyone knows anything about anything," said Bear to himself, "it's Owl who knows something about something," he said, "or my name's not Winnie-the-Pooh," he said. "Which it is," he added. "So there you are."

Owl lived at The Chestnuts, an old-world residence of great charm, which was grander than anybody else's, or seemed so to Bear, because it had both a knocker *and* a bell-pull. Underneath the knocker there was a notice which said:

PLES RING IF AN RNSER IS REQIRD

Underneath the bell-pull there was a notice which said:

PLEZ CNOKE IF AN RNSR IS NOT REQID.

These notices had been written by Christopher Robin, who was the only one in the forest who could spell; for Owl, wise though he was in many ways, able to read and write and spell his own name WOL, yet somehow went all to pieces over delicate words like MEASLES and BUTTEREDTOAST.

Winnie-the-Pooh read the two notices very carefully, first from left to right, and afterwards, in case he had missed some of it, from right to left. Then, to make quite sure, he knocked and pulled the knocker, and he pulled and knocked the bell-rope, and he called out in a very loud voice, "Owl! I require an answer! It's Bear speaking." And the door opened, and Owl looked out.

"Hallo, Pooh," he said. "How's things?"

"Terrible and Sad," said Pooh, "because Eeyore, who is a friend of mine, has lost his tail. And he's Moping about it. So could you very kindly tell me how to find it for him?"

"Well," said Owl, "the customary procedure in such cases is as follows."

"What does Crustimoney Proseedcake mean?" said Pooh. "For I am a Bear of Very Little Brain, and long words Bother me."

"It means the Thing to Do."

"As long as it means that, I don't mind," said Pooh humbly.

"The thing to do is as follows. First, Issue a Reward. Then —"

"Just a moment," said Pooh, holding up his paw. "*What* do we do to this - what you were saying? You sneezed just as you were going to tell me."

"I *didn't* sneeze."

"Yes, you did, Owl."

"Excuse me, Pooh, I didn't. You can't sneeze without knowing it."

"Well, you can't know it without something having been sneezed."

"What I *said* was, 'First *Issue* a Reward'."

"You're doing it again," said Pooh sadly.

"A Reward!" said Owl very loudly. "We write a notice to say that we will give a large something to anybody who finds Eeyore's tail."

"I see, I see," said Pooh, nodding his head. "Talking about large somethings," he went on dreamily, "I generally have a small something about now - about this time in the morning," and he looked wistfully at the cupboard in the corner of Owl's parlour; "just a mouthful of condensed milk or what-not, with perhaps a lick of honey —"

"Well, then," said Owl, "we write out this notice, and we put it up all over the Forest."

"A lick of honey," murmured Bear to himself, "or – or not, as the case may be." And he gave a deep sigh, and tried very hard to listen to what Owl was saying.

But Owl went on and on, using longer and longer words, until at last he came back to where he started, and he explained that the person to write out this notice was Christopher Robin.

"It was he who wrote the ones on my front door for me. Did you see them, Pooh?"

For some time now Pooh had been saying "Yes" and "No" in turn, with his eyes shut, to all that Owl was saying, and having said, "Yes, yes," last time, he said, "No, not at all," now, without really knowing what Owl was talking about.

"Didn't you see them?" said Owl, a little surprised. "Come and look at them now."

So they went outside. And Pooh looked at the knocker and the notice below it, and he looked at the bell-rope and the notice below it, and the more he looked at the bell-rope, the more he felt that he had seen something like it, somewhere else, sometime before.

"Handsome bell-rope, isn't it?" said Owl.

Pooh nodded."It reminds me of something," he said, "but I can't think what. Where did you get it?"

"I just came across it in the Forest. It was hanging over a bush, and I thought at first somebody lived there, so I rang it, and nothing happened, and then I rang it again very loudly, and it came off in my hand, and as nobody seemed to want it, I took it home, and —"

"Owl," said Pooh solemnly, "you made a mistake. Somebody did want it."

"Who?"

"Eeyore. My dear friend Eeyore. He was – he was fond of it."

"Fond of it?"

"Attached to it," said Winnie-the-Pooh sadly.

* * * * *

So with these words he unhooked it, and carried it back to Eeyore; and when Christopher Robin had nailed it on in its right place again, Eeyore frisked about the forest, waving his tail so happily that Winnie-the-Pooh came over all funny, and had to hurry home for a little snack of something to sustain him. And, wiping his mouth half

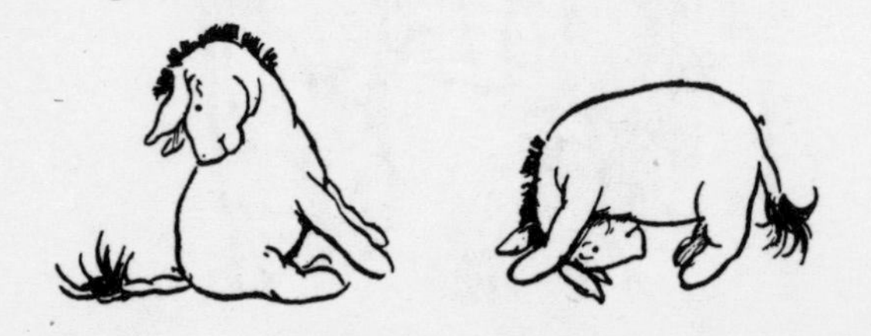

an hour afterwards, he sang to himself proudly:

Who found the Tail?
"I," said Pooh,
"At a quarter to two
(Only it was quarter to eleven really),
I found the Tail!"

The Three Foxes

Once upon a time there were three little foxes
Who didn't wear stockings, and they didn't wear sockses,
But they all had handkerchiefs to blow their noses,
And they kept their handkerchiefs in cardboard boxes.

They lived in the forest in three little houses,
And they didn't wear coats and they didn't wear trousies.
They ran through the woods on their little bare tootsies,
And they played "Touch last" with a family of mouses.

They didn't go shopping in the High Street shopses,
But caught what they wanted in the woods and copses.
They all went fishing, and they caught three wormses,
They went out hunting, and they caught three wopses.

They went to a Fair and they all won prizes –
Three plum-puddingses and three mince-pieses.
They rode on elephants and swang on swingses,
And hit three coco-nuts at coco-nut shieses.

That's all I know of the three little foxes
Who kept their handkerchiefs in cardboard boxes.
They lived in the forest in three little houses,
But they didn't wear coats and they didn't wear trousies.
And they didn't wear stockings and they didn't wear sockses.

Solitude

I have a house where I go
  When there's too many people,
I have a house where I go
  Where no one can be;
I have a house where I go,
Where nobody ever says "No"
Where no one says anything – so
  There is no one but me.

In which a house is built at Pooh Corner for Eeyore

One day when Pooh Bear had nothing else to do, he thought he would do something, so he went round to Piglet's house to see what Piglet was doing. It was still snowing as he stumped over the white forest track, and he expected to find Piglet warming his toes in front of his fire, but to his surprise he saw that the door was open, and the more he looked inside the more Piglet wasn't there.

"He's out," said Pooh sadly. "That's what it is. He's not in. I shall have to go a fast Thinking Walk by myself. Bother!"

But first he thought that he would knock very loudly just to make *quite* sure . . . and while he waited for Piglet not to answer, he jumped up and down to keep warm, and a hum came suddenly into his head, which seemed to him a Good Hum, such as is Hummed Hopefully to Others.

The more it snows
(Tiddely pom),
The more it goes
(Tiddely pom),
The more it goes
(Tiddely pom),
On snowing.
And nobody knows
(Tiddely pom),

How cold my toes
(Tiddely pom),
How cold my toes
(Tiddely pom),
Are growing.

"So what I'll do," said Pooh, "is I'll do this. I'll just go home first and see what the time is, and perhaps I'll put a muffler round my neck, and then I'll go and see Eeyore and sing it to him."

He hurried back to his own house; and his mind was so busy on the way with the hum that he was getting ready for Eeyore that, when he suddenly saw Piglet sitting in his best arm-chair, he could only stand there rubbing his head and wondering whose house he was in.

"Hallo, Piglet," he said. "I thought you were out."

"No," said Piglet, "it's you who were out, Pooh."

"So it was," said Pooh. "I knew one of us was."

He looked up at his clock, which had stopped at five minutes to eleven some weeks ago.

"Nearly eleven o'clock," said Pooh happily. "You're just in time for a little smackerel of something," and he put his head into the cupboard. "And then we'll go out, Piglet, and sing my song to Eeyore."

"Which song, Pooh?"

"The one we're going to sing to Eeyore," explained Pooh.

The clock was still saying five minutes to eleven when Pooh and Piglet set out on their way half an hour later. The wind had dropped, and the snow, tired of rushing round in circles trying to catch itself up, now fluttered gently down until it found a place on which to rest, and sometimes the place was Pooh's nose and sometimes it wasn't, and in a little while Piglet was wearing a white muffler round his neck and feeling more snowy behind the ears than he had ever felt before.

"Pooh," he said at last, and a little timidly, because he didn't want Pooh to think he was Giving In, "I was just wondering. How would it be if we went home now and *practised* your song, and then sang it to Eeyore to-morrow – or – or the next day, when we happen to see him?"

"That's a very good idea, Piglet," said Pooh. "We'll practise it now as we go along. But it's no good going home to practise it, because it's a special Outdoor Song which Has To Be Sung In The Snow."

"Are you sure?" asked Piglet anxiously.

"Well, you'll see, Piglet, when you listen. Because this is how it begins. *The more it snows, tiddely pom –*"

"Tiddely what?" said Piglet.

"Pom," said Pooh. "I put that in to make it more hummy. *The more it goes, tiddely pom, the more –*"

"Didn't you say snows?"

"Yes, but that was *before*."

"Before the tiddely pom?"

"It was a *different* tiddely pom," said Pooh, feeling rather muddled now. "I'll sing it to you properly and then you'll see."

So he sang it again.

The more it
SNOWS - tiddely-pom
The more it
GOES - tiddely-pom
The more it
GOES - tiddely-pom
On
Snowing.

And nobody
KNOWS - tiddely-pom,
How cold my
TOES - tiddely-pom
How cold my
TOES - tiddely-pom
Are
Growing.

He sang it like that, which is much the best way of singing it, and when he had finished, he waited for Piglet to say that, of all the Outdoor Hums for Snowy Weather he had ever heard, this was the best. And, after thinking the matter out carefully, Piglet said:

"Pooh," he said solemnly, "it isn't the *toes* so much as the *ears*."

By this time they were getting near Eeyore's Gloomy Place, which was where he lived, and as it was still very snowy behind Piglet's ears, and he was getting tired of it, they turned into a little pine-wood, and sat down on the gate which led into it. They were out of the snow now, but it was very cold, and to keep themselves warm they sang Pooh's song right through six times, Piglet doing the tiddely-poms and Pooh doing the rest of it, and both of them thumping on the top of the gate with pieces of stick at the proper places. And in a little while they felt much warmer, and were able to talk again.

"I've been thinking," said Pooh, "and what I've been thinking about is this. I've been thinking about Eeyore."

"What about Eeyore?"

"Well, poor Eeyore has nowhere to live."

"Nor he has," said Piglet.

"*You* have a house, Piglet, and I have a house, and they are very good houses. And Christopher Robin has a house, and Owl and Kanga and Rabbit have houses, and even Rabbit's friends and relations have houses or somethings, but poor Eeyore has nothing. So what I've been thinking is: Let's build him a house."

"That," said Piglet, "is a Grand Idea. Where shall we build it?"

"We will build it here," said Pooh, "just by this wood, out of the wind, because this is where I thought of it. And we will call this Pooh Corner. And we will build an Eeyore House with sticks at Pooh Corner for Eeyore."

"There was a heap of sticks on the other side of the wood," said Piglet, "I saw them. Lots and lots. All piled up."

"Thank you, Piglet," said Pooh. "What you have just said will be a Great Help to us, and because of it I could call this place Poohanpiglet Corner if Pooh Corner didn't sound better, which it does, being smaller and more like a corner. Come along."

So they got down off the gate and went round to the other side of the wood to fetch the sticks.

Christopher Robin had spent the morning indoors going to Africa and back, and he had just got off the boat and was wondering what it was like outside, when who should come knocking at the door but Eeyore.

"Hallo, Eeyore," said Christopher Robin, as he opened the door and came out. "How are *you*?"

"It's snowing still," said Eeyore gloomily.

"So it is."

"*And* freezing."

"Is it?"

"Yes," said Eeyore. "However," he said, brightening up a little, "we haven't had an earthquake lately."

"What's the matter, Eeyore?"

"Nothing, Christopher Robin. Nothing important. I suppose you haven't seen a house or what-not anywhere about?"

"What sort of a house?"

"Just a house."

"Who lives there?"

"I do. At least I thought I did. But I suppose I don't. After all, we can't all have houses."

"But, Eeyore, I didn't know – I always thought —"

"I don't know how it is, Christopher Robin, but what with all this snow and one thing and another, not to mention icicles and such-like, it isn't so Hot in my field about three o'clock in the morning and as people think it is. It isn't Close, if you know what I mean – not so as to be uncomfortable. It isn't Stuffy. In fact, Christopher Robin," he went on in a loud whisper, "quite-between-ourselves-and-don't-tell-anybody, it's Cold."

"Oh, Eeyore!"

"And I said to myself: The others will be sorry if I'm getting myself all cold. They haven't got Brains, any of them, only grey fluff that's blown into their heads by mistake, and they don't Think, but if it goes on snowing for another six weeks or so, one of them will begin to say to himself: 'Eeyore can't be so very much too Hot about three o'clock in the morning.' And then it will Get About. And they'll be Sorry."

"Oh, Eeyore!" said Christopher Robin, feeling very sorry already.

"I don't mean you, Christopher Robin. You're different. So what it all comes to is that I built myself a house down by my little wood."

"Did you really? How exciting!"

"The really exciting part," said Eeyore in his most melancholy voice, "is that when I left it this morning it was there, and when I came back it wasn't. Not at all, very natural, and it was only Eeyore's house. But still I just wondered."

Christopher Robin didn't stop to wonder. He was already back in *his* house, putting on his waterproof hat, his waterproof boots, and his waterproof macintosh as fast as he could.

"We'll go and look for it at once," he called out to Eeyore.

"Sometimes," said Eeyore, "when people have quite finished taking a person's house, there are one or two bits which they don't want and are rather glad for the person to take back, if you know what I mean. So I thought if we just went —"

"Come on," said Christopher Robin, and off they hurried, and in a very little time they got to the corner of the field by the side of the pine-wood, where Eeyore's house wasn't any longer.

"There!" said Eeyore. "Not a stick of it left! Of course, I've still got all this snow to do what I like with. One mustn't complain."

But Christopher Robin wasn't listening to Eeyore, he was listening to something else.

"Can you hear it?" he asked.

"What is it? Somebody laughing?"

"Listen."

They both listened . . . and they heard a deep gruff voice saying in a singing voice that the more it snowed the more it went on snowing, and a small high voice tiddely-pomming in between.

"It's Pooh," said Christopher Robin excitedly . . .

"Possibly," said Eeyore.

"*And* Piglet!" said Christopher Robin excitedly.

"Probably," said Eeyore. "What we *want* is a Trained Bloodhound."

The words of the song changed suddenly.

"We've finished our HOUSE!" sang the gruff voice.
"Tiddely pom!" sang the squeaky one.
"It's a beautiful HOUSE . . ."
"Tiddely pom . . ."
"I wish it were MINE . . ."
"Tiddely pom . . ."

"Pooh!" shouted Christopher Robin . . .

The singers on the gate stopped suddenly.

"It's Christopher Robin!" said Pooh eagerly.

"He's round by the place where we got all those sticks from," said Piglet.

"Come on," said Pooh.

They climbed down their gate and hurried round the corner of the wood, Pooh making welcoming noises all the way.

"Why, here *is* Eeyore," said Pooh, when he had finished hugging Christopher Robin, and he nudged Piglet, and Piglet nudged him, and they thought to themselves what a lovely surprise they had got ready. "Hallo, Eeyore."

"Same to you, Pooh Bear, and twice on Thursdays," said Eeyore gloomily.

Before Pooh could say: "Why Thursdays?" Christopher Robin began to explain the sad story of Eeyore's Lost House. And Pooh and Piglet listened, and their eyes seemed to get bigger and bigger.

"*Where* did you say it was?" asked Pooh.

"Just here," said Eeyore.

"Made of sticks?"

"Yes."

"Oh!" said Piglet.

"What?" said Eeyore.

"I just said 'Oh!'" said Piglet nervously. And so as to seem quite at ease he hummed tiddely-pom once or twice in a what-shall-we-do-now kind of way.

"You're sure it was a house?" said Pooh. "I mean, you're sure the house was just here?"

"Of course I am," said Eeyore. And he murmured to himself, "No brain at all, some of them."

"Why, what's the matter, Pooh?" asked Christopher Robin.

"Well," said Pooh . . . "The fact *is,*" said Pooh . . . "Well, the fact is," said Pooh . . . "You see," said Pooh . . . "It's like this," said Pooh, and something seemed to tell him that he wasn't explaining very well, and he nudged Piglet again.

"It's like this," said Piglet quickly . . . "Only warmer," he added after deep thought.

"What's warmer?"

"The other side of the wood, where Eeyore's house is."

"*My* house?" said Eeyore. "My house was here."

"No," said Piglet firmly. "The other side of the wood."

"Because of being warmer," said Pooh.

"But I ought to *know* —"

"Come and look," said Piglet simply, and he led the way.

"There wouldn't be *two* houses," said Pooh. "Not so close together."

They came round the corner, and there was Eeyore's house, looking as comfy as anything.

"There you are," said Piglet.

"Inside as well as outside," said Pooh proudly.

Eeyore went inside . . . and came out again.

"It's a remarkable thing," he said. "It is my house, and I built it where I said I did, so the wind must have blown it here. And the wind blew it right over the wood, and blew it down here, and here it is as good as ever. In fact, better in places."

"Much better," said Pooh and Piglet together.

"It just shows what can be done by taking a little trouble," said Eeyore. "Do you see, Pooh? Do you see, Piglet? Brains first and then Hard Work. Look at it! *That's* the way to build a house," said Eeyore proudly.

So they left him in it; and Christopher Robin went back to lunch with his friends Pooh and Piglet, and on the way they told him of the Awful Mistake they had made. And when he had finished laughing, they all sang the Outdoor Song for Snowy Weather the rest of the way home, Piglet, who was still not quite sure of his voice, putting in the tiddely-poms again.

"And I know it *seems* easy," said Piglet to himself, "but it isn't *every one* who could do it."

The Engineer

Let it rain!
Who cares?
I've a train upstairs,
With a brake
Which I make
From a string
Sort of thing,
Which works
In jerks,
'Cos it drops
In the spring,
Which stops
With the string,

And the wheels
All stick
So quick
That it feels
Like a thing
That you make
With a brake,
Not string. . . .

So that's what I make,
When the day's all wet.
It's a good sort of brake
But it hasn't worked yet.

Waiting at the Window

These are my two drops of rain
Waiting on the window-pane.

I'm waiting here to see
Which the winning one will be.

Both of them have different names.
One is John and one is James.

All the best and all the worst
Comes from which of them is first.

James has just begun to ooze.
He's the one I want to lose.

John is waiting to begin.
He's the one I want to win.

James is going slowly on.
Something sort of sticks to John.

John is moving off at last.
James is going pretty fast.

John is rushing down the pane.
James is going slow again.

James has sort of met a smear.
John is getting very near.

Is he going fast enough?
(James has met a bit of fluff.)

John has hurried quickly by.
(James was talking to a fly.)

John is there, and John has won!
Look! I told you! Here's the sun!

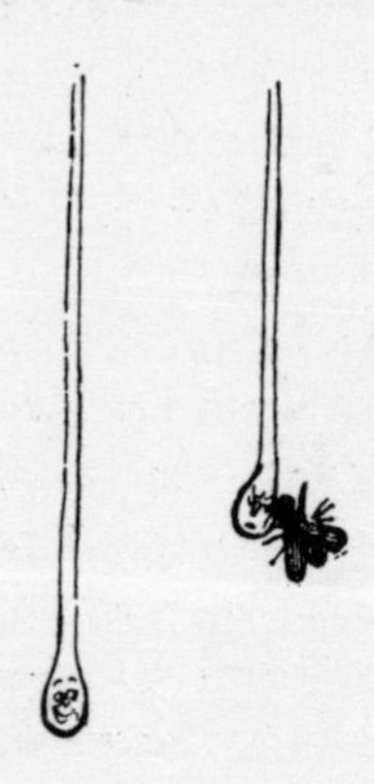

In which Pooh invents a new game and Eeyore joins in

By the time it came to the edge of the Forest the stream had grown up, so that it was almost a river, and, being grown-up, it did not run and jump and sparkle along as it used to do when it was younger, but moved more slowly. For it knew now where it was going, and it said to itself, "There is no hurry. We shall get there some day." But all the little streams higher up in the Forest went this way and that, quickly, eagerly, having so much to find out before it was too late.

There was a broad track, almost as broad as a road, leading from the Outland to the Forest, but before it could come to the Forest, it had to cross this river. So, where it crossed, there was a wooden bridge, almost as broad as a road, with wooden rails on each side of it. Christopher Robin could just get his chin on to the top rail, if he wanted to, but it was more fun to stand on the bottom rail, so that he could lean right over, and watch the river slipping slowly away beneath him. Pooh could get his chin on to the bottom rail if he wanted to, but it was more fun to lie down and get his head under it, and watch the river slipping slowly away beneath him. And this was the only way in which Piglet and Roo could watch the river at all, because they were too small to reach the bottom rail. So they would lie down and watch it . . . and it slipped away very slowly, being in no hurry to get there.

One day, when Pooh was walking towards this bridge, he was trying to make up a piece of poetry about

fir-cones, because there they were, lying about on each side of him, and he felt singy. So he picked a fir-cone up, and looked at it, and said to himself, "This is a very good fir-cone, and something ought to rhyme to it." But he couldn't think of anything. And then this came into his head suddenly:

Here is a myst'ry
About a little fir-tree.
Owl says it's *his* tree,
And Kanga says it's *her* tree.

"Which doesn't make sense," said Pooh, "because Kanga doesn't live in a tree."

He had just come to the bridge; and not looking where he was going, he tripped over something, and the fir-cone jerked out of his paw into the river.

"Bother," said Pooh, as it floated slowly under the bridge, and he went back to get another fir-cone which had a rhyme to it. But then he thought that he would just look at the river instead, because it was a peaceful sort of day, so he lay down and looked at it, and it slipped slowly away beneath him . . . and suddenly, there was his fir-cone slipping away too.

"That's funny," said Pooh. "I dropped it on the other side," said Pooh, "and it came out on this side! I wonder if it would do it again?" And he went back for some more fir-cones.

It did. It kept on doing it. Then he dropped two in at once, and leant over the bridge to see which of them would come out first; and one of them did; but as they were both the same size, he didn't know if it was the one which he wanted to win, or the other one. So the next time he dropped one big one and one little one, and the big one came out first, which was what he had said it would do, and the little one came out last, which was what he had said it would do, so he had won twice . . . and when he went home for tea, he had won thirty-six and lost twenty-eight, which meant that he was – that he had – well, you take twenty-eight from thirty-six, and *that's* what he was. Instead of the other way round.

And that was the beginning of the game called Poohsticks, which Pooh invented, and which he and his friends used to play on the edge of the Forest. But they played with sticks instead of fir-cones, because they were easier to mark.

Now one day Pooh and Piglet and Rabbit and Roo were all playing Poohsticks together. They had dropped their sticks in when Rabbit said "Go!" and then they had hurried across to the other side of the bridge, and now they were all leaning over the edge, waiting to see whose stick would come out first. But it was a long time coming, because the river was very lazy that day, and hardly seemed to mind if it didn't ever get there at all.

"I can see mine!" cried Roo. "No, I can't, it's something else. Can you see yours, Piglet? I thought I could see mine, but I couldn't. There it is! No, it isn't. Can you see yours, Pooh?"

"No," said Pooh.

"I expect my stick's stuck," said Roo. "Rabbit, my stick's stuck. Is your stick stuck, Piglet?"

"They always take longer than you think," said Rabbit.

"How long do you *think* they'll take?" asked Roo.

"I can see yours, Piglet," said Pooh suddenly.

"Mine's a sort of greyish one," said Piglet, not daring to lean too far over in case he fell in.

"Yes, that's what I can see. It's coming over on to my side."

Rabbit leant over further than ever, looking for his, and Roo wriggled up and down, calling out "Come on, stick! Stick, stick, stick!" and Piglet got very excited because his was the only one which had been seen, and that meant that he was winning.

"It's coming!" said Pooh.

"Are you *sure* it's mine?" squeaked Piglet excitedly.

"Yes, because it's grey. A big grey one. Here it comes! A very – big – grey – Oh, no, it isn't, it's Eeyore."

And out floated Eeyore.

"Eeyore!" cried everybody.

Looking very calm, very dignified, with his legs in the air, came Eeyore from beneath the bridge.

"It's Eeyore!" cried Roo, terribly excited.

"Is that so?" said Eeyore, getting caught up by a little eddy, and turning slowly round three times. "I wondered."

"I didn't know you were playing," said Roo.

"I'm not," said Eeyore.

"Eeyore, what are you doing there?" said Rabbit.

"I'll give you three guesses, Rabbit. Digging holes in the ground? Wrong. Leaping from branch to branch of a young oak-tree? Wrong. Waiting for somebody to help me out of the river? Right. Give Rabbit time, and he'll always get the answer."

"But Eeyore," said Pooh in distress, "what can we – I mean, how shall we – do you think if we —"

"Yes," said Eeyore. "One of those would be just the thing. Thank you, Pooh."

"He's going *round* and *round*," said Roo, much impressed.

"And why not?" said Eeyore coldly.

"I can swim too," said Roo proudly.

"Not round and round," said Eeyore. "It's much more difficult. I didn't want to come swimming at all today," he went on, revolving slowly. "But if, when in, I decide to practise a slight circular movement from right to left– or perhaps I should say, "he added, as he got into another eddy, "from left to right, just as it happens to occur to me, it is nobody's business but my own." There was a moment's silence while everybody thought.

"I've got a sort of idea," said Pooh at last, "but I don't suppose it's a very good one."

"I don't suppose it is either," said Eeyore.

"Go on, Pooh," said Rabbit. "Let's have it."

"Well, if we all threw stones and things into the river on *one* side of Eeyore, the stones would make waves, and the waves would wash him to the other side."

"That's a very good idea," said Rabbit, and Pooh looked happy again.

"Very," said Eeyore. "When I want to be washed, Pooh, I'll let you know."

"Supposing we hit him by mistake?" said Piglet anxiously.

"Or supposing you missed him by mistake," said Eeyore. "Think of all the possibilities, Piglet, before you settle down to enjoy yourselves."

But Pooh had got the biggest stone he could carry, and was leaning over the bridge, holding it in his paws.

"I'm not throwing it, I'm dropping it, Eeyore," he explained. "And then I can't miss - I mean I can't hit you. *Could* you stop turning round for a moment, because it muddles me rather?"

"No," said Eeyore. "I *like* turning round."

Rabbit began to feel that it was time he took command.

"Now, Pooh," he said, "when I say 'Now!' you can drop it. Eeyore, when I say 'Now!' Pooh will drop his stone."

"Thank you very much, Rabbit, but I expect I shall know."

"Are you ready, Pooh? Piglet, give Pooh a little more room. Get back a bit there, Roo. Are you ready?"

"No," said Eeyore.

"*Now*!" said Rabbit.

Pooh dropped his stone. There was a loud splash, and Eeyore disappeared . . .

It was an anxious moment for the watchers on the bridge. They looked and looked . . . and even the sight of Piglet's stick coming out a little in front of Rabbit's didn't cheer them up as much as you would have expected. And then, just as Pooh was beginning to think that he must have chosen the wrong stone or the wrong river or the wrong day for his Idea, something grey showed for a moment by the river bank . . . and it got slowly bigger and bigger . . . and at last it was Eeyore coming out.

With a shout they rushed off the bridge, and pushed and pulled at him; and soon he was standing among them again on dry land.

"Oh, Eeyore, you *are* wet!" said Piglet, feeling him.

Eeyore shook himself, and asked somebody to explain to Piglet what happened when you had been inside a river for quite a long time.

"Well done, Pooh," said Rabbit kindly. "That was a good idea of ours."

"What was?" asked Eeyore.

"Hooshing you to the bank like that."

"*Hooshing* me?" said Eeyore in surprise. "Hooshing *me*? You didn't think I was hooshed, did you? I dived. Pooh dropped a large stone on me, and so as not to be struck heavily on the chest, I dived and swam to the bank."

"You didn't really," whispered Piglet to Pooh, so as to comfort him.

"I didn't *think* I did," said Pooh anxiously.

"It's just Eeyore," said Piglet. "I thought your Idea was a very good Idea."

Pooh began to feel a little more comfortable, because when you are a Bear of Very Little Brain, and you Think of Things, you find sometimes that a Thing which seemed very Thingish inside you is quite different when it gets out into the open and has other people looking at it. And, anyhow, Eeyore was in the river, and now he wasn't, so he hadn't done any harm.

"How did you fall in, Eeyore?" asked Rabbit, as he dried him with Piglet's handkerchief.

"I didn't," said Eeyore.

"But how –"

"I was BOUNCED," said Eeyore.

"Oo," said Roo excitedly, "did somebody push you?"

"Somebody BOUNCED me. I was just thinking by the side of the river – thinking, if any of you know what that means – when I received a loud BOUNCE."

"Oh, Eeyore?" said everybody.

"Are you sure you didn't slip?" asked Rabbit wisely.

"Of course I slipped. If you're standing on the slippery bank of a river, and somebody BOUNCES you loudly from behind, you slip. What did you think I did?"

"But who did it?" asked Roo.

Eeyore didn't answer.

"I expect it was Tigger," said Piglet nervously.

"But, Eeyore," said Pooh, "was it a Joke, or an Accident? I mean —"

"I didn't stop to ask, Pooh. Even at the very bottom of the river I didn't stop to say to myself, '*Is* this a Hearty Joke, or is it the Merest Accident?' I just floated to the surface, and said to myself, 'It's wet.' If you know what I mean."

"And where was Tigger?" asked Rabbit.

Before Eeyore could answer, there was a loud noise behind them, and through the hedge came Tigger himself.

"Hallo, everybody," said Tigger cheerfully.

"Hallo, Tigger," said Roo.

Rabbit became very important suddenly.

"Tigger," he said solemnly, "what happened just now?"

"Just when?" said Tigger a little uncomfortably.

"When you bounced Eeyore into the river."

"I didn't bounce him."

"You bounced me," said Eeyore gruffly.

"I didn't really. I had a cough, and I happened to be

behind Eeyore, and I said '*Grr-oppp-ptschschschz.*'"

"Why?" said Rabbit, helping Piglet up, and dusting him. "It's all right, Piglet."

"It took me by surprise," said Piglet nervously.

"That's what I call bouncing," said Eeyore. "Taking people by surprise. Very unpleasant habit. I don't mind Tigger being in the Forest, " he went on, "because it's a large Forest, and there's plenty of room to bounce in it. But I don't see why he should come into *my* little corner of it, and bounce there. It isn't as if there was anything very wonderful about my little corner. Of course for people who like cold, wet, ugly bits it *is* something rather special, but otherwise it's just a corner, and if anybody feels bouncy –"

"I didn't bounce, I coughed," said Tigger crossly.

"Bouncy or Coffy, it's all the same at the bottom of the river."

"Well," said Rabbit, "all I can say is – well, here's Christopher Robin, so *he* can say it."

Christopher Robin came down from the Forest to the bridge, feeling all sunny and careless, and just as if twice nineteen didn't matter a bit, as it didn't on such a happy afternoon, and he thought that if he stood on the bottom rail of the bridge, and leant over, and watched the river slipping slowly away beneath him, then he would suddenly know everything that there was to be known, and he would be able to tell Pooh, who wasn't quite sure about some of it. But when he got to the bridge and saw all the animals there, then he knew that it wasn't that kind of afternoon, but the other kind, when you wanted to *do* something.

"It's like this, Christopher Robin," began Rabbit, "Tigger —"

"No, I didn't," said Tigger.

"Well, anyhow, there I was," said Eeyore.

"But I don't think he meant to," said Pooh.

"He just *is* bouncy," said Piglet, "and he can't help it."

"Try bouncing *me,* Tigger," said Roo eagerly. "Eeyore, Tigger's going to try *me*. Piglet, do you think —"

"Yes, yes," said Rabbit, "we don't all want to speak at once. The point is, what does Christopher Robin think about it?"

"All I did was I coughed," said Tigger.

"He bounced," said Eeyore.

"Well, I sort of boffed," said Tigger.

"Hush!" said Rabbit, holding up his paw. "What does Christopher Robin think about it all? That's the point."

"Well," said Christopher Robin, not quite sure what it was all about. "*I* think —"

"Yes?" said everybody.

"*I* think we all ought to play Poohsticks."

So they did. And Eeyore, who had never played it before, won more times than anybody else; and Roo fell in twice, the first time by accident and the second time on purpose, because he suddenly saw Kanga coming from the Forest, and he knew he'd have to go to bed anyhow. So then Rabbit said he'd go with them; and Tigger and Eeyore went off together, because Eeyore wanted to tell Tigger How to Win at Poohsticks, which you do by letting your stick drop in a twitchy sort of way, if you understand what I mean, Tigger; and Christopher Robin and Pooh and Piglet were left on the bridge by themselves.

For a long time they looked at the river beneath them, saying nothing, and the river said nothing too, for it felt very quiet and peaceful on this summer afternoon.

"Tigger is all right, *really*," said Piglet lazily.

"Of course he is," said Christopher Robin.

"Everybody is *really*," said Pooh. "That's what I think," said Pooh. "But I don't suppose I'm right," he said.

"Of course you are." said Christopher Robin.

The Wisdom of Pooh

In Celebration of Winnie-the-Pooh's Seventy-fifth Anniversary

PUBLISHED APRIL 2001

0416199291 The Hums of Pooh *p/b*
by A.A.Milne illustrated by E.H.Shepard

PUBLISHED SEPTEMBER 2001

0416199194 Wisdom from Pooh *h/b*
0416199208 Courage from Piglet *h/b*
0416199216 Thoughts from Eeyore *h/b*
0416199224 Cheer from Tigger *h/b*

Tiny format Gift Books inspired by A.A.Milne and illustrated by E.H.Shepard

PUBLISHED OCTOBER 2001

0416199178 Three Cheers for Pooh *h/b*
A Celebration of the Bear of Very Little Brain
by Brian Sibley

Fully illustrated in colour and black and white

The Wisdom of Pooh

Titles inspired by A.A.Milne and illustrated by E.H. Shepard

Pooh on Philosophy

0416195113 The Tao of Pooh *p/b*
0416195121 The Te of Piglet *p/b*
0416195261 The Tao of Pooh & The Te of Piglet *p/b*
by Benjamin Hoff

0749320702 Pooh and the Philosophers *p/b*
0416197973 Pooh and the Second Millennium *p/b*
(A paperback edition of Pooh and the Ancient Mysteries)
0416198171 Pooh and the Psychologists *h/b*
by John Tyerman Williams

0416194915 The Pooh Book of Quotations *p/b*
Compiled by Brian Sibley

074932290X The Pooh Dictionary *p/b*
by A.R. Melrose

Pooh on Management

0413697207 Winnie-the-Pooh on Management *p/b*
0413707105 Winnie-the-Pooh on Problem Solving *p/b*
041619513X Winnie-the-Pooh on Management & Problem Solving *p/b*
0416195563 Winnie-the-Pooh on Success *p/b*
by Roger E. Allen and Stephen D. Allen

Pooh on Life

041619656X Winnie-the-Pooh's Little Book of Wisdom *p/b*
0416196772 Eeyore's Little Book of Gloom *p/b*
0416196764 Tigger's Little Book of Bounce *p/b*
0416196500 Winnie-the-Pooh's Little Book of Feng Shui *p/b*

Latin Editions

0416194893 Winnie ille Pu *p/b*
by Alexander Lenard
0416194907 Domus Anguli Puensis *p/b*
by Brian Gerrard Staples

A. A. Milne's Classic Books illustrated by E.H.Shepard

Classic Colour Hardback Editions

0416168604	Winnie-the-Pooh
0416789005	The House at Pooh Corner
0416152627	When We Were Very Young
0416153127	Now We Are Six
0416168426	The Winnie-the-Pooh Collection Box Set
0416188435	Winnie-the-Pooh The Complete Collection of Stories and Poems

Classic Black and White Paperback Editions

0749702109	Winnie-the-Pooh
0749701161	The House at Pooh Corner
0749702095	When We Were Very Young
0749702087	Now We Are Six
0749720255	The World of Pooh Collection Box Set

Classic Colour Paperback Editions

0749707100	Winnie-the-Pooh
0740707119	The House at Pooh Corner
0749711809	When We Were Very Young
0749711795	Now We Are Six
0749711817	Pooh Gift Box Set